This igloo book belongs to:

....

igloobooks

Published in 2019
by Igloo Books Ltd
Cottage Farm
Sywell
NN6 0BJ
www.igloobooks.com

GOL002 0319
6 8 10 9 7
ISBN 978-1-78810-152-3

Written by Stephanie Moss
Illustrated by Katya Longhi

Designed by Justine Ablett
Edited by Stephanie Moss

Printed and manufactured in China

The Day I Met a
Monster

igloobooks

One day, I met a monster.

He jumped out and said,

"BOO!"

"Hello," I said, calmly.

"I'm Sally. Who are you?"

He smiled a cheeky grin and wiped away some monster **drool.**

Then before I knew it, the monster followed me to school!

He got me into **trouble**
when I took my spelling test.
I got one answer right,
but he **ruined** all the rest!

He hid under the table and ate **noisily** at lunch.
The monster was so **messy**, chewing loudly...

... **Munch,**

crunch,

munch!

By the afternoon, I had really had enough.

He made my teacher angry by going through her stuff!

When it was time for ballet, I was sure that he would quit. But whoever knew that monsters could do a perfect split?

"**Help!**" I cried to Lily, when I was at her house to play.
"**The monster I met this morning won't seem to go away!**"

The monster **jumped** onto the table when it was time for tea. I couldn't help but **yell** out at him,

"PLEASE, STOP FOLLOWING ME!"

It was all getting too much.

The monster was everywhere.

I was close to **screaming** and then **tearing** out my hair!

That night, as I sat in bed, I knew I needed to have a plan.
"I have to get rid of the monster," I thought, **"any way I can!"**

I introduced him to my brother.
They'd be **best** friends, for sure!
But when the monster broke his toys,
he wouldn't play with him any more.

I thought I'd try the dog instead,
as they both **slobber** and **smell**.

But the monster **gobbled** up his dinner...

... so Smudge grew
tired of him as well.

After those disasters, he did more than follow me round.

The monster **stamped** his feet...

... and **dragged** his knuckles on the ground.

He threw **smelly** stuff everywhere.

He **dug** holes in the road.

One day, he got so angry,
I thought he might

explOde!

So I sat down with the monster
and as I looked into his eyes,
he said his first words to me
and it took me by **surprise.**

"I don't want to scare anyone," he said, "like other monsters do.

The only person I've made friends with in a while, Sally, is you."

This whole time he hadn't scared me.
I hadn't even heard him

roar.

Then I saw the other monsters.
I'd never felt so lucky before.

"I'm so sorry, Monster," I said.
"I didn't understand."
Then I leaned towards him and
took him by the hand.

Monster **jumped** up in the air and he grinned his toothy smile.

Then he grabbed me in the **biggest** hug I'd had in quite a while!

Now we are the **best** of friends, Monster never feels sad.

In fact, Monster is the most fun friend I think I've **ever** had!